ONE DAY IN MAY

by Kitty Colton

illustrated by Kyrsten Brooker

HOUGHTON MIFFLIN BOSTON

Spring had come to the city. At least the calendar said so. There it was, in big, bold letters: May.

But when Lin looked out her window, everything looked gray.

She saw no trees bursting with pale green buds. No candy-colored flowers poking through the ground. No bluebirds carrying twigs and leaves to line their nests. Not even a black-and-yellow bee.

All she saw was gray. Gray walls and gray roofs. Gray streets and gray steam rising from the grates. A patch of gray sky between the tall gray buildings.

She went outside, sat on her gray stoop, and sighed. She thought about spring at her old home, in the country. “I wish we’d never moved to the city,” she said to her gray cat, Cleo.

A fat tear rolled down Lin’s cheek. Cleo leaped off the stoop to chase a pigeon.

"My, my, you look like a storm cloud," said a sunny voice. Lin looked up, startled. A woman was sitting on the tree stump in front of her building.

"Huh?" Lin said, wiping her eyes. The city was crowded with people. But she had never seen anyone like this.

The woman's eyes gleamed like pieces of blue sea glass. Her hair was piled up like a bird's nest, woven with twigs and leaves. Her skirt was a deep velvety green, soft as the mossy floor of the forest.

Cleo stopped chasing the pigeon and stared. (Being a cat, she didn't care about being rude.) Then, to Lin's horror, Cleo jumped straight onto the woman's head.

“Oh!” Lin cried out, laughing. “I’m sorry. Cleo, you get down from there, you bad cat.” But Cleo was already half buried in the woman’s tangled mass of hair.

“No, that’s purrrrr-fectly fine,” the woman replied calmly, as if animals jumped into her hair all day long.

Lin remembered that she was in a very bad mood. She started to scowl again.

"Tell me what's troubling you on such a lovely day," the woman said. Just then, the pigeon landed on her shoulder. "Helloooo!" she cooed at it.

“It’s not a lovely day at all!” Lin said. “I hate the city. Back where I used to live, spring meant flowers and birds and blue sky. Here everything is just gray and dead.”

The pigeon squawked loudly. “He says, ‘What’s wrong with gray?’” the woman told Lin. Cleo poked her head out and meowed her agreement.

Lin shrugged and kicked at the stump.

"You shouldn't kick trees," the woman said gently. "They have feelings too, you know."

"But it's just a dead stump!" Lin said, and she kicked it again because that was the mood she was in.

The woman jumped to her feet and pointed down. A branch had sprouted up where she was sitting.

"Sometimes you don't notice what's right in front of your nose," she said.

Lin folded her arms stubbornly.

"Or what's right outside your window," the woman added. She pointed to a pile of gray twigs perched on Lin's building.

Lin heard a faint chirp, chirp. Suddenly a large bird swooped down to the ledge, and the chirps grew louder. "A nest of baby falcons," the woman said. Cleo's eyes grew round as moons.

"Nature isn't just bright colors," said the woman. "Gray has its place too. Without gray skies and rain, there would be no flowers. And no worms to feed the baby birds."

She paused and then added, half to herself, "But maybe there *has* been too much rain lately."

Just then, a bright burst of sun made Lin shade her eyes. Neighbors appeared on their stoops. They smiled and lifted their heads to the warmth, contented as Cleo.

"It really is spring!" Lin said. She ran up the stairs and into her house. She grabbed her brother, who was in front of his computer, as always.

"But I don't want to go outside!" he cried as they reached the doorway. "It's just a dumb old gray—"

The streets were soaked with sunshine. The city was bursting with the colors and sounds of spring.

Lin looked for her new friend, but she was gone. A patch of pink tulips had sprouted in her place. Cleo lay beside them, licking her sun-warmed fur.